The Library Store presents . . .

The Adventures Begin

By Jen Jellyfish, M.M.

Illustrated by Kurt Keller and Traci Van Wagoner

Special thanks to . . .

TLS
THE LIBRARY STORE®

To Riley

Steve

Greg

Dale

Jen Jellyfish

To Bobby and Hannah with love, love, love! —Mom
And to Aundi and Jim, owners of The Chick-Inn;
in memory of their son (my nephew) Ben. —Aunt Jen

In memory of
Kyle Gunter and Ben Woolard,
whisked from our arms into heaven
too young. We miss you.
We'll see you again!

First Edition

Presented by The Library Store
P.O. Box 0964, Tremont, IL 61568
www.thelibrarystore.com

Special thanks to Sara McDonnell, Layout Designer, The Library Store.

Archway Publishing books may be ordered through booksellers or by contacting:

Archway Publishing
1663 Liberty Drive
Bloomington, IN 47403
www.archwaypublishing.com
1 (888) 242-5904

ISBN: 978-1-4808-3879-6 (sc)
ISBN: 978-1-4808-3881-9 (hc)
ISBN: 978-1-4808-3880-2 (e)

Print information available on the last page.

Archway Publishing rev. date: 02/02/2017

Welcome to beautiful Juneberry Square, hometown of the AD-VEN-TUR-OUS Booker T. Bear.

Booker's Grandpop and Grandmop own the Bee-Nutty shop. They make BEE snacks with nuts on top. There's Beebee, Freebee, and Frisbee snacks, Honeybee, Wannabee, and even Zombee snacks.

Meet Booker's best friend, Dahlya Dragonfly.
She likes adventures of a very STRANGE kind.

Pronounced DOLL-ya.

YUUUM! Words crunch!

She likes to find WEIRD, JUICY words to eat,
and serves them at her diner—
as if the words were TREATS!

DAHLYA'S DINER

Long and fat words like
EN-TO-MOL-OGY.

The study about ME!

Booker calls her The Weird Word Queen.
When she hears the nickname, she spreads her wings and PREENS.
He says, "Dahlya is the PRIS-SI-EST insect I've seen!
But she likes to go AD-VEN-TUR-ING around the world with me!"

Just off the square is the Bear Family den.
By the den, in the yard with the hens, is The Chick-Inn.

Booker has white, black, and speckled hens.
They peck food from the ground and lay eggs in the inn.

Booker and Grandpop built The Chick-Inn,
in memory of Grandpop's brother, Booker's great-uncle Ben.

Grandpop and Uncle Ben were I-DEN-TI-CAL TWINS.
Not only that, they were adventurous best friends!
Grandpop had traveled to EXCITING places with Ben.

"Come inside! I'll show you our home.
We love our books as much as honeycombs.
You may be wondering what's on our globe.
I stuck a bright STICKY on every place
I want to go: Australia, Greenland . . .
even the Congo! Who knows, maybe I'll
travel to the icy North Pole!"

"The photos Grandmop arranged in our den are
all the STU-PEN-DOUS places
Grandpop and Uncle Ben have been!"

Grandmop called out, "It's suppertime. Come!"

"Are you HungAry?" Grandpop asked Booker, laughing at the pun.

Magpie, Booker's dog, thought Grandmop had called her too.
She ran FAST to the table for a turkey bone to chew.

"Some countries sound like supper!" Grandpop pointed to TUR-KEY.

YUUUM! Ge-og-ra-phy!

Turkey

"Yes they do," Grandmop laughed. "Grab your spoon, there's CHI-LE!"

"What about PIZZA?" Booker searched with appetite.

"I've eaten pizza in a *piAzza*." Grandpop pinned Sicily with his knife.

PiAzza is pronounced pea-AHT-zah.

Sicily

Booker's peas went flying as he jumped up EC-STAT-I-CAL-LY.
"I'm going to the piAzza," he shouted, "to eat pizza in Sicily!"

"I have to pack my backpack!" he hurried,
knocking over the lemon tree.
"But first I have to make a list
of all the things I'll need!"

"OH NO! My Jet-Away jacket is missing from its hook!"

It was the MOST IMPORTANT thing, so they all began to look.

Booker looked behind his bedroom door.
Dahlya searched EVERYWHERE, from ceiling to floor.

Grandpop and Grandmop were searching cabinets and bins
when Dahlya suggested . . .

But the Jet-Away jacket was not with the hens.

Everyone had searched EVERYWHERE.
They had searched all around.
But Booker's Jet-Away jacket was NOWHERE to be found!

Booker cringed.

The jacket had been Great-Grandpop's.
He had given it to the twins.
Then, when Booker turned ten,
Grandpop had passed it on to him.

It was an ancient bear tradition
to pass the jacket down.
But it still looked BRAND NEW—
a shiny leather brown.

Grandpop had said to Booker with a twinkling, sparkling glow,
"Although this jacket looks brand new, it's more than 100 CEN-TUR-IES old!
This jacket will take you on FAN-TAS-TI-CAL adventures,
WHEREVER you want to go."

As the ancient story has always been told,
an old 'Magination Maker had stitched it with PURE GOLD!
Strands of yellow, white, and shiny red rose!

Then the old 'Magination Maker had THUN-DER-OUS-LY foretold:
"Imagination magic will NEVER grow old!"

The jacket was Booker's most VALUED possession.
Now it was MISSING! And they were all out of guesses.

They searched again, beginning with the brass hook.
The jacket was not there, so they continued to look.

It was not behind Booker's bedroom door.

It was not anywhere on his bedroom floor.

It was not in a cabinet. It was not in a bin.
It was not with the hens, or in The Chick-Inn.

Can YOU guess where they finally found it??

Beneath Magpie's rear end!

With everything gathered they were ready to roll.
Booker shouted, "To Sicily for pizza at the PIAZZA!"

Let's GO!

Booker put on his Jet-Away jacket and cap.
He put on his backpack, his arms through the straps.
They squeezed their eyes shut, spread arms and wings wide,
and together they shouted . . .

To Sicily! To Sicily!
To SICILY!
Let's FLY!

When they opened their eyes they saw a MAG-NIF-I-CENT elephant fountain.
And in the distance stood Mt. Etna, a huge VOLCANO mountain!
Booker snapped photos of monuments and tombs.

Dahlya liked the sweet-smelling plumeria in bloom.

They saw palace thrones,
red cathedral domes,
and ancient bridges of stone.

Still they were not tired. They continued to roam.
They wanted pizza from the piAzza before they jetted home.

Atop a crusty old building in Duomo Square,
they saw a crusty old sign that read:

PAPA'S
PIAZZA PIZZA
YOU ARE HERE!

RAV-EN-OUS-LY hungry, they were heading for the door
when the earth began to RUMBLE and Mt. Etna ERUPTED with a ROAR!

"WATCH OUT!" shrieked Booker as a rain of fiery ash began to pour.
They made a quick dash for the pizza café door.

When they entered the café, safe from the storm,
they were warmly greeted by an UN-U-SU-AL life-form.

"Ben-ve-nu-ti!" he sang.
"That means WELCOME in Italian.
Today's pizza is Blue Cheese topped with
SCRUMP-TIOUS red scallion!"

Booker and Dahlya had never met a living ROCK.
Booker was so FAS-CI-NAT-ED, he could hardly talk.
But he managed to share,
"We're hungry adventurers from Juneberry Square.
This is my friend Dahlya, and I'm Booker T. Bear."

The rock lit up, "My name is Tuff."
He handed them each a wide coffee cup.
"I'm from Mt. Etna. That's where I was formed,
on a day like today, from a hot lava storm."

Tuff told volcano stories while Booker and Dahlya ate.
Then he served them a warm mountain
of molten lava cake.

"YUUUM," said Booker. "Sicily has great taste!"

What an amazing adventure Sicily had been.
But like all great adventures,
their journey was coming to an end . . . . .

It was time to return to Juneberry Square.
Booker's Jet-Away jacket would return them safely there.

Back in Dahlya's Diner everyone had nestled in.
The two best friends listed all the places they had been,
and talked EX-CIT-ED-LY about Tuff, their new Italian friend.

Booker said, "I have SOOO many stories to write.
I'd better get started in my Travel Journal tonight."

Grandmop smiled brightly as she listened with joy.
Grandpop said, "Your Jet-Away jacket has much MORE in store!"

With a grin on his face and a happy ROAR,
Booker said to Dahlya, "There's a WHOLE WORLD to explore!"

DAHLYA'S DINER

OPEN 24/7!   EVERY DAY: BOOK BUFFET!

Tuff is a real rock type. Tuff forms when a volcano spews hot liquid rocks, minerals, and glass from its mouth *(YIKES!)* into the sky!

When the wet, sticky elements fall to Earth, they get stuck together and form various colors, funny shapes, and different sizes called *tuff rock.*

As tuff cools, it becomes hard. Tuff can form as small rocks and huge boulders. Some tuff mountains have caves and tunnels!

You can find tuff rock formations in Sicily and all around the world—wherever volcanoes have erupted.

Weird Word Stew—Try a few!

entomology [en-to-mol-o-gy] — the scientific study of insects, like Dahlya Dragonfly! Entomology is a branch of zoology. Zoology is the study of the animal kingdom, which includes bears (like Booker, Grandpop, and Grandmop), and dogs (like Magpie).

Magpie [mag-pie] — a person or animal who collects anything they find, for no reason at all, whether a bone, a paper clip, a leaf . . . , or a Jet-Away jacket! That's why Booker's dog is named Magpie.

preen — to clean up, dress up, have good hygiene, and take pride in your achievements—like Booker and Dahlya! When you hear "preen" think "clean."

plumeria [plu-me-ri-a] — a flower that smells spicy and sweet. The women of Sicily used to give plumeria to their daughters and granddaughters after marriage, to decorate their new homes.

scallion [scal-lion] — a small onion bulb with a long green stem. The bulb is commonly white, but there are also red scallions. Like all onions, scallions can taste hot!

You'll find Dahlya's yummy **Molten Lava Cake** recipe at Dahlya's Diner online: www.BookerTBear.com

TODAY'S SPECIAL

Papa's Piazza Pizza

You'll need:
- A round or wide baking pan—like a pizza pan or cookie sheet
- 1 medium flour or corn tortilla, or other flat bread
- 2-4 tbsp. pizza sauce or Alfredo sauce
- 1/8 cup shredded mozzarella cheese
- 1/8 cup finely crumbled/chopped blue cheese, if you please
- 1 tbsp. finely grated Parmesan cheese

Optional: A finely chopped scallion (both stem and bulb), and your favorite pizza toppings

Directions:
1. Preheat oven to 425°.
2. Place tortilla (or other flat bread) on a baking pan.
3. Spread sauce evenly over the tortilla.
4. Sprinkle with mozzarella cheese.
5. Top with just a few scallions and/or other toppings of your choosing. *(Booker likes meat and Dahlya likes veggies. Grandmop and Grandpop like both!)*
6. Sprinkle with blue cheese, if you please.
7. Sprinkle with Parmesan cheese.
8. Bake for 8-10 minutes. Check after 8 minutes. *YUUUM!*

Visit Booker, Dahlya, and Friends
in Juneberry Square online at
www.BookerTBear.com

There's lots of fun in Juneberry Square!

In the Toy & Book Shop you can:

- Order Booker T. Bear™ books
- Preview and pre-order upcoming Booker T. Bear™ books
- Order the Booker T. Bear™ Travel Journal
- Order the Booker T. Bear™ plush toy

In Dahlya's Diner you can:

- Print Dahlya's yummy recipes
- Print a free coloring page
- Find big, juicy words to munch and more!

In Juneberry Square you can also:

- Get the latest news about book signing events
- Learn more about the author and illustrators and connect with them
- Learn more about the many characters in Booker T. Bear™ books and more!

CPSIA information can be obtained
at www.ICGtesting.com
Printed in the USA
LVOW06s2128200217
524871LV00001B/1/P